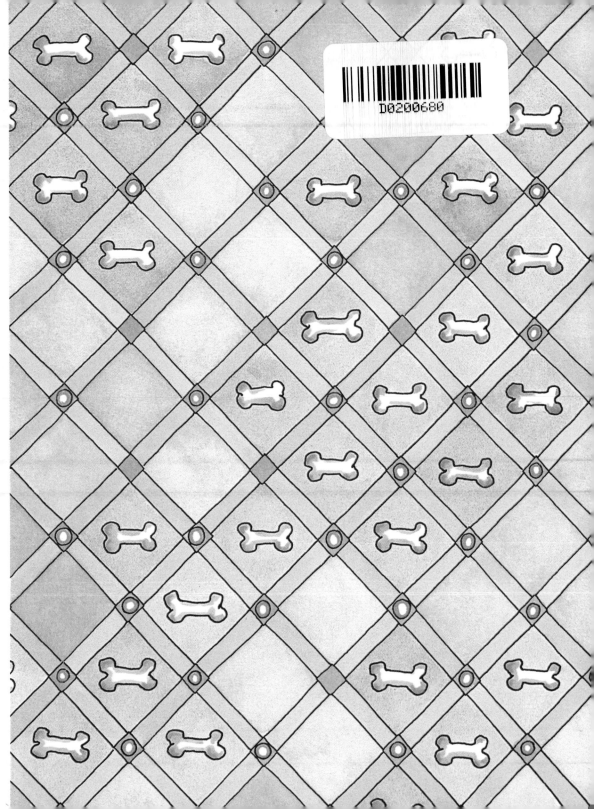

A Parents Magazine
Read Aloud Original

Where's Rufus?

Where's Rufus?

by Stephanie Calmenson
pictures by Maxie Chambliss

Publication licensed by Gruner + Jahr USA Publishing

LIBRARY OF CONGRESS
Library of Congress Cataloging-in-Publication Data

Calmenson, Stephanie.
Where's Rufus? / by Stephanie Calmenson; pictures by Maxie
Chambliss.
p.   cm.
Summary: The Plinketts' dog Rufus hides throughout the house to
delay their departure on a picnic, because only he knows that it is
starting to rain outside. While family members search for him, the
reader is asked to find where he is.
ISBN 0-8193-1177-4
[1. Dogs—Fiction. 2. Picnicking—Fiction. 3. Literary
recreations.] I. Chambliss, Maxie, ill. II. Title.
PZ7.C136Wi   1988
[E]—dc 19   88-4092
                                                          CIP
                                                           AC

To Anthony and Paul Johnson—S.C.

For Michelle and Matt Hoey
with love and dog biscuits—M.C.

"Rise and shine!" said Mr. Plinkett.
"The sun is shining.
It is a perfect day for a picnic."
"Hurray!" said Lucy and Sam.
"Ga, ga," said Baby.
"Woof!" said Rufus.

At breakfast, the Plinketts
planned what they would bring.
"Peanut butter and jelly
sandwiches," said Sam.
"Fizzy-Fizz to drink," said Lucy.

While they were talking,
Rufus was looking out the window.
He saw a small, gray rain cloud.
He wanted to tell
the Plinketts about it.

"Woof!" barked Rufus.
"Hush, Rufus," said Mrs. Plinkett.
"We can't think with so much noise."

But Rufus saw another
rain cloud rolling in.
"Woof! Woof!" he barked,
louder than before.
"Down, boy," said Mr. Plinkett.

When Rufus saw one more rain cloud,
he knew it was *not*
a good time for a picnic.

"Www-oof! Www-oof!" howled Rufus.
But he could not get
the Plinketts to turn around.

After breakfast, when Mr. and Mrs. Plinkett
were filling the food basket,
Rufus tried to stop them.

And when Lucy and Sam
were packing their toys,
Rufus tried to take the toys away.

Finally, the Plinketts were ready to go.
Rufus had to think of a new way
to keep them inside.
So, he hid.
"Here, Rufus," called Lucy.
But Rufus didn't come.
"Rufus!" called Sam. "It's time to go."
"Maybe we should leave without him,"
said Mr. Plinkett.
"NO!" cried Lucy and Sam.
"A picnic without Rufus
would be no fun at all!"
Rufus was happy to hear that.

Sam went to the living room
to look for Rufus.
He looked behind the bookcase.
He looked under the couch.
He looked behind the curtains.
But he didn't find Rufus.

Do you know where Rufus is?

Rufus raced into the kitchen.
Lucy went there to look for him.
She looked under the table.
She looked in the closet.
She even looked in the refrigerator.
But she didn't find Rufus.

Do you know where Rufus is?

Rufus got to the bathroom
just in time to hide.
Mrs. Plinkett looked behind the door.
She looked in the bathtub.
She looked under the sink.
But she didn't find Rufus.

Do you know where Rufus is?

Mr. Plinkett went into the den.
He looked under the desk.
He looked behind the television.
He looked behind the chair.
But he didn't find Rufus.

Do you know where Rufus is?

On the way to Baby's room,
Rufus passed a window and
looked outside.
"Someday they will thank me
for this," he thought.

Baby toddled into her room.
She looked under her crib.
She looked into her toy box.
She looked behind her giraffe.
But she didn't find Rufus.

Do you know where Rufus is?

Suddenly, there was
a crash of thunder.
Rufus jumped into Baby's arms.
"Doggie!" said Baby.

"Good for you, Baby!" said Lucy.
"You found Rufus!"
"Wow! Look at all that rain!" said Sam,
pointing out the window.

The Plinketts waited
for the rain to stop.
When the sun was shining again,
they went on their picnic.

"It's a good thing we didn't leave
when we planned," said Mr. Plinkett.
"We can thank Rufus for that,"
said Lucy.

"Woof! Woof!" barked Rufus.
He was always glad to help.

About the Author

Stephanie Calmenson is the author of many popular books for children, including *Ten Furry Monsters* and *The Giggle Book,* which were illustrated by Maxie Chambliss. Before turning to writing full-time, she was an elementary school teacher and a children's book editor. Ms. Calmenson grew up in Brooklyn, New York, and now lives in Manhattan.

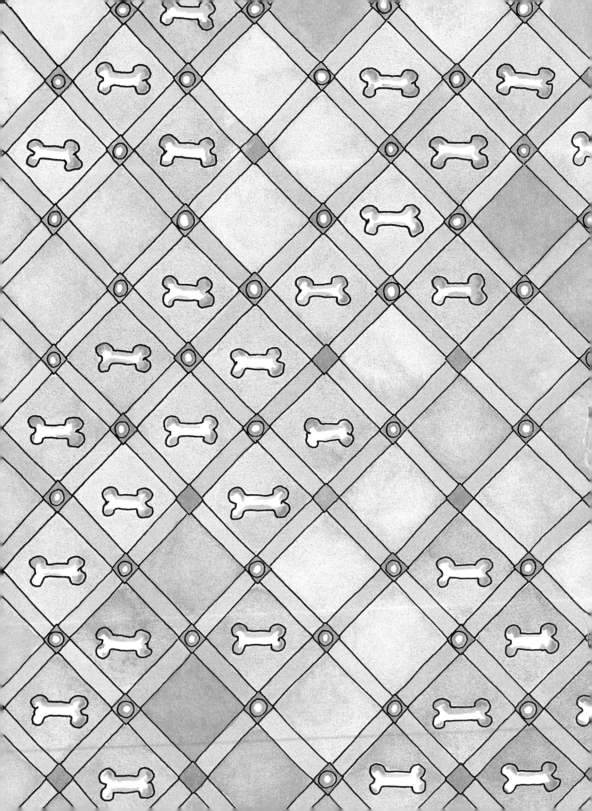